SNIP AND CLIP

Created by
Steven A. Johnson

First published in Great Britain in 2017 by

Garden Barber Ltd
P.O. Box 23,
Hertford,
Hertfordshire SG14 3PZ

© Steven A. Johnson 2017

ISBN 978-0-9529962-6-2

Buttercup sat close to where the two **bears** hug in Kensington Gardens.

She was reading a story about **kings** and queens and thought, "Nothing exciting ever happens to me. I'd **love** to meet a real king or **queen.**"

As if by **magic,**
Snip and Clip appeared in front of her.
They come from an amazing world
called Garden Barber Land.

"Is this **really** happening to me?"
cried Buttercup, smiling at the

two friendly **bugs.**

Snip, Clip and Buttercup
stood by the Lucombe oak tree.

"Oh my goodness... I can't believe it.

Snip and Clip and **me!**

Can we go on an **adventure?"**
Buttercup smiled.

"Well," said Snip,
"what do you think, Clip?"

"Are you here just for me?"
asked Buttercup. "Take me to
Garden Barber Land, please,
Snip... **Please!**"

Clip **smiled**
and said, "We are going to take you on
an **adventure,** Buttercup."

They turned to the Lucombe oak
and **knocked** on the trunk
three times.

Buttercup closed her **eyes**
and said under her breath,

"YES!"

There was **whizzing** and a **whooshing,** a **flash** and a **pop**!

"Good morning to you," said the large old oak tree. **"Welcome** to Garden Barber Land." **"Wow!"** said Buttercup. "Good morning to you too!"

"Everything lives in **harmony** here.
It was all created by Mr Garden,
the most perfect gardener,"
said Clip.

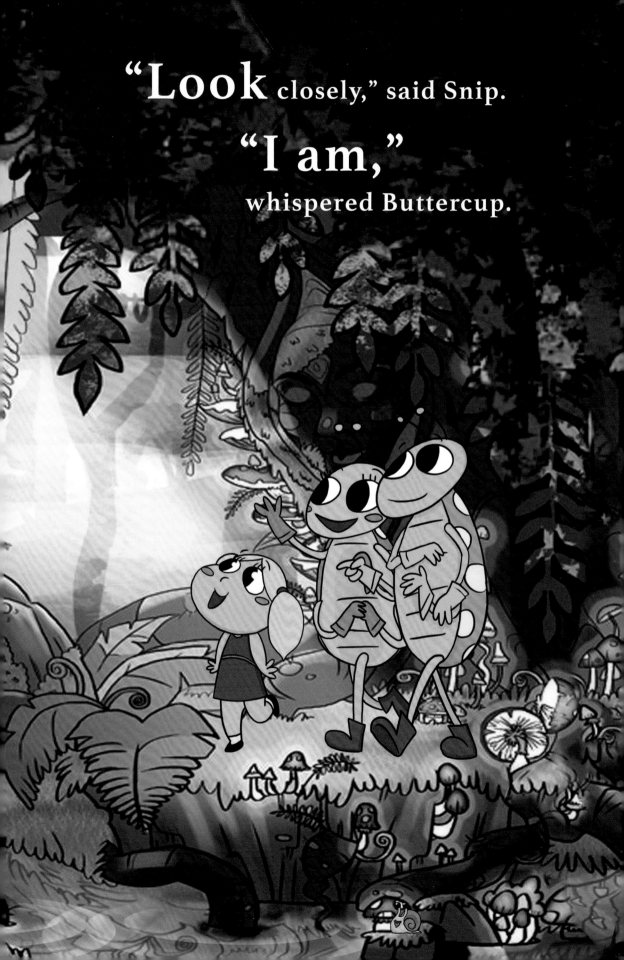

"**Look** closely," said Snip.

"**I am,**"
whispered Buttercup.

All of a sudden, Mr Garden appeared.
"There is work that needs to be
done at Buckingham Palace,"
he said.

"Oh, gosh,
Buckingham
Palace!"
gasped Buttercup.
"Can I help?"

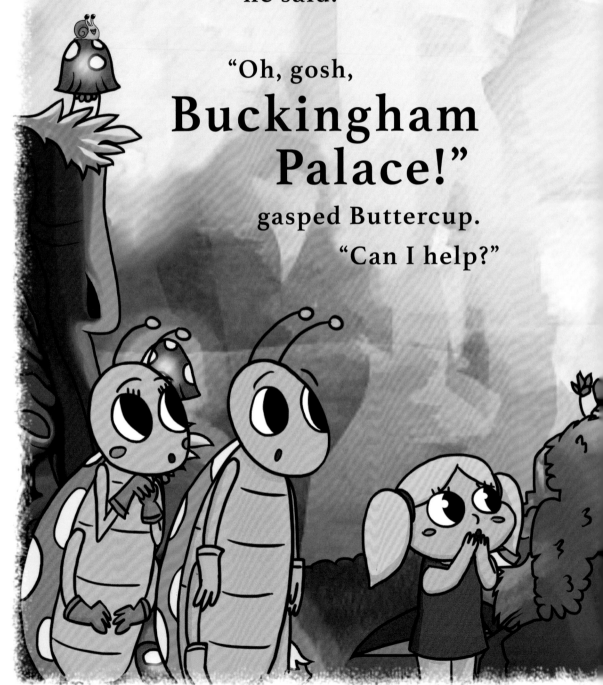

"Yes! You must all go –
at once!"

said Mr Garden.

"Can I take a **selfie** before we go?"
asked Buttercup.
As quickly as he could, the oak tree
took a picture for Buttercup.

Then they knocked three times on the trunk of the old oak. There was a **whizzing** and a **whooshing,** a **flash** and a **pop!**

They were outside Buckingham Palace!
The **wind** had damaged the gardens.

"What can be done?" asked Buttercup.

"It's awfully **sad.**"

"We'll show you," said Snip.

"You can help," said Clip.

With a *whizzing* and a *whooshing,* a *flash* and a *pop,* the gardens were transformed.

A voice called from the palace window, "That looks **better!** I must come down and thank you!"

Buttercup was **brimming** with **pride.** "Are you the King?" she shouted.

"Ermm... well..."

"This is Buttercup, our friend," said Clip.

"I've read stories about kings and queens but I've never met a real king or queen. Are you the **King?**" asked Buttercup.

"Ermm... well... It's been quite an adventure for you my dear, I'm sure..."

"Oh gosh, I can't wait to tell my mum!" Buttercup smiled.

"Thank you, Snip and Clip,
I've had such a wonderful time.
Goodbye for now."
Snip and Clip gave her a **hug.**

"Before you go," said Clip, "here is a **special** magical gift from Garden Barber Land, just for you."

Buttercup stared at the **magic** seed. **"Wow!** Thank you," she said.

When Buttercup got home, she raced to
find her mum.

"Mum! Mum! You won't believe what
happened today!

Snip and Clip came to Kensington Gardens
and we went on an **adventure**
to Garden Barber Land...

Mr Garden sent us to Buckingham Palace
where I helped Snip and Clip
tidy the gardens...

Then I met the King – at least, I think
it was the King, although he didn't say.

They gave me this seed!"

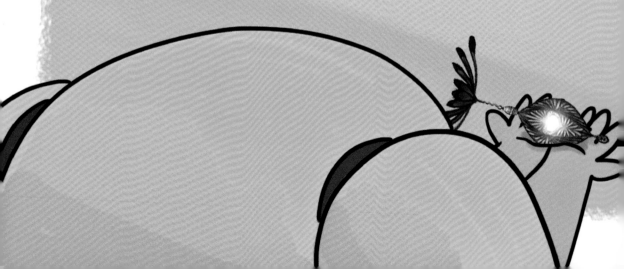

"Oh Buttercup,
your imagination is so
WILD!"
said Mum.

Later, Buttercup lay on her bed.

"Maybe Mum was right," she thought.

"It must have been a **dream.**"

She **sighed** and muttered to herself,

"Nothing exciting

ever

happens to me...

It was just a

dream."

Then Buttercup
remembered something.

"My **phone!**" she screamed.
"Mum! Mum! Look! It must be **true!**
Here are Snip and Clip!

I must have met the
King!"

The end.

Did you spot **Sonny**, the snail,
on every page?